For Deborah
~ DB

For my daughter, Kirsten
~ GH

LITTLE TIGER PRESS
An imprint of Magi Publications
1 The Coda Centre, 189 Munster Road, London SW6 6AW
www.littletigerpress.com
This paperback edition published in 2002
First published in Great Britain 2001
Text © 2001 David Bedford • Illustrations © 2001 Gaby Hansen
David Bedford and Gaby Hansen have asserted their rights
to be identified as the author and illustrator of this work
under the Copyright, Designs and Patents Act, 1988.
Printed in Italy by Grafiche AZ, Verona
All rights reserved • ISBN 1 85430 719 3
1 2 3 4 5 6 7 8 9 10

THIS LITTLE TIGER BOOK BELONGS TO:

_____

_____

_____

_____

David Bedford *and* Gaby Hansen

# Big Bears Can!

LITTLE TIGER PRESS
London

Big Bear had to look after
Little Bear when Mummy
Bear went out.
"Do I have to?" asked Big Bear.
"Yes," said Mummy Bear.
"Just keep the house tidy.
I won't be long."

"What can Big Bears do?" asked Little Bear
when Mummy Bear had gone.
"Big Bears can do *everything*," said Big Bear.
"Can they stand on their heads?"
"Yes they can," said Big Bear.

*"See!"*

"But they can't do *this*," said Little Bear . . .

BOING! BOING!
"Of course they can,"
said Big Bear.
"That's easy."

BOING, BOING, BOING...

*"Oops!"*

"Can you fix the springs?"
asked Little Bear.
"Yes," said Big Bear.
"I can."

"But you can't do *this*,"
said Little Bear. "No way."

"Big Bears don't swing," said
Big Bear. "That would be silly."
"You're too big to swing,
anyway," said Little
Bear.

"NO I'M NOT," roared Big Bear. "Watch this!"

"Look out!"
said Little Bear.
"You're too heavy!"

"You've squashed Mummy's
flowers, too," said Little Bear.
"Can you fix everything?"
"I *hope* I can," said Big Bear.

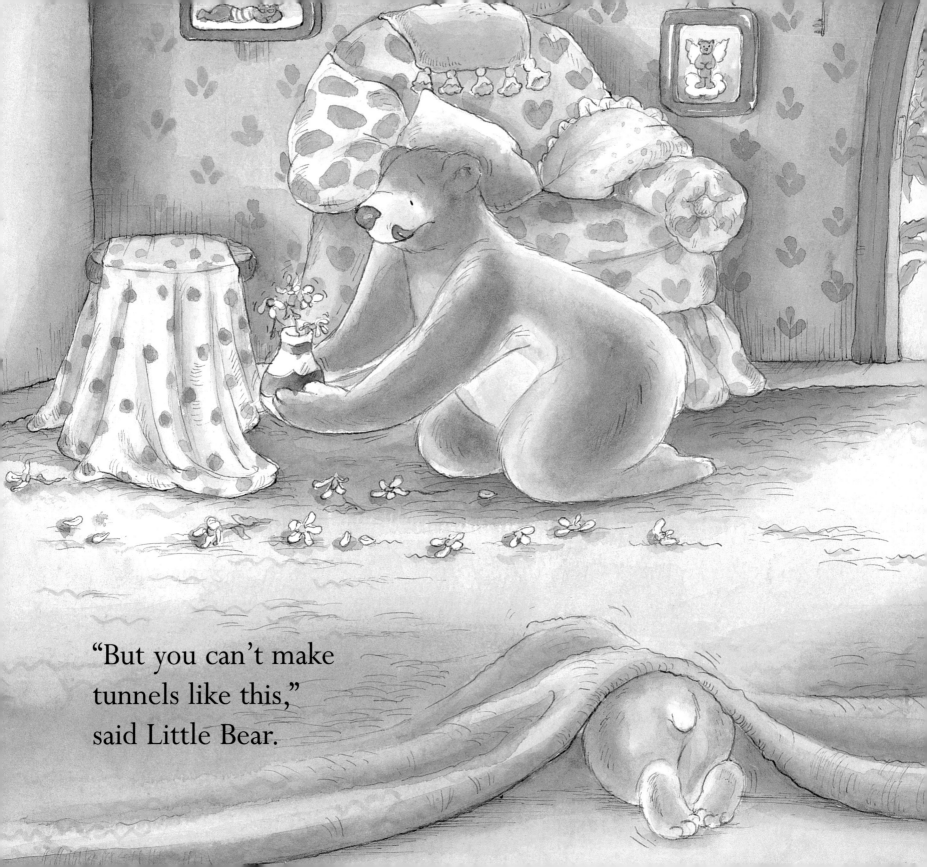

"But you can't make
tunnels like this,"
said Little Bear.

"I don't want to make tunnels," said Big Bear. "I'm going to sit quietly until Mummy comes back."

"Big Bears *can't* do everything," sang Little Bear. "Big Bears *can't*, Big Bears *can't*, Big Bears CAN'T do everything."
"YES THEY CAN!" said Big Bear.

"This is fun, isn't it!" said Big Bear.
"HERE COMES MUMMY," shouted
Little Bear. "She's going to be very angry."

"Big Bears can't hide," said
Little Bear.
"Yes they can," said Big Bear.
"Move over so I can squeeze
in beside you."
"There's not enough room,"
said Little Bear. "Mummy
will see you."

"Look at Mummy's face," said Little Bear.
"She's very, very, VERY angry."
"Big Bears can't get told off," whispered
Big Bear. "Can they?"

YES THEY CAN!

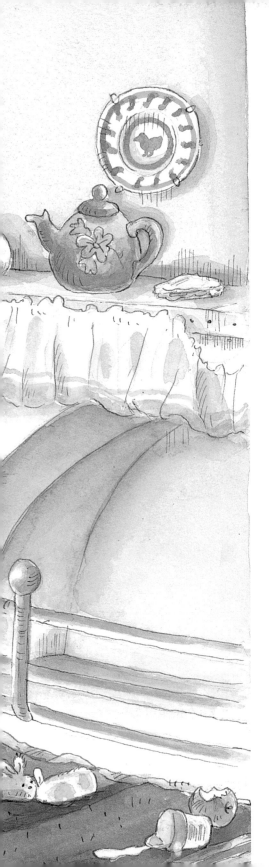

Poor Big Bear. If only Little Bear could make him feel better.
"Can Big Bears have hugs?" asked Little Bear.

"Yes," said Big Bear.

"Big Bears can!"

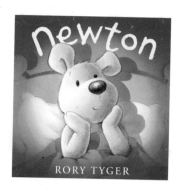
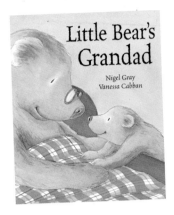
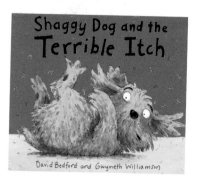
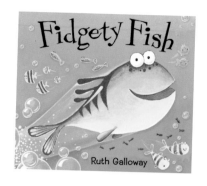

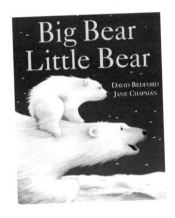

# More books for big bears and little bears to share

For information regarding the above titles or for our catalogue, please contact us: Little Tiger Press, 1 The Coda Centre, 189 Munster Road, London SW6 6AW

Telephone: 020 7385 6333 • Fax: 020 7385 7333

e-mail: info@littletiger.co.uk • www.littletigerpress.com